For Cathy – P.H.

Text copyright © Kathryn Cave 2013
Illustrations copyright © Paul Hess 2013

The right of Kathryn Cave to be identified as author and of Paul Hess
to be identified as illustrator of this work has been asserted by them in accordance with
the Copyright, Designs and Patents Act, 1988 (United Kingdom).

First published in Great Britain and in the USA in 2013 by
Frances Lincoln Children's Books, 4 Torriano Mews,
Torriano Avenue, London NW5 2RZ

www.frances-lincoln.com

A catalogue record for this book is available from the British Library.

ISBN 978-1-84780-238-5

Illustrated with watercolours

Set in Bell Gothic

Printed in Dongguan, Guangdong, China by Toppan Leefung

1 3 5 7 9 8 6 4 2

TROLL
WOOD

KATHRYN CAVE

Illustrated by
PAUL HESS

F

FRANCES LINCOLN
CHILDREN'S BOOKS

This is Troll Wood.
No one goes there.
Will you?

"We will."

And they did.

There's no path through the wood.
It was lost long ago.
Will you find it?

"We will."

And they did.

Deep in the wood there are trees
with apples and plums.
No one eats them.
Will you?

"We will."

And they did.

There's a hill in the wood
where wild flowers grow.
No one climbs it.
Will you?

"We will."

And they did.

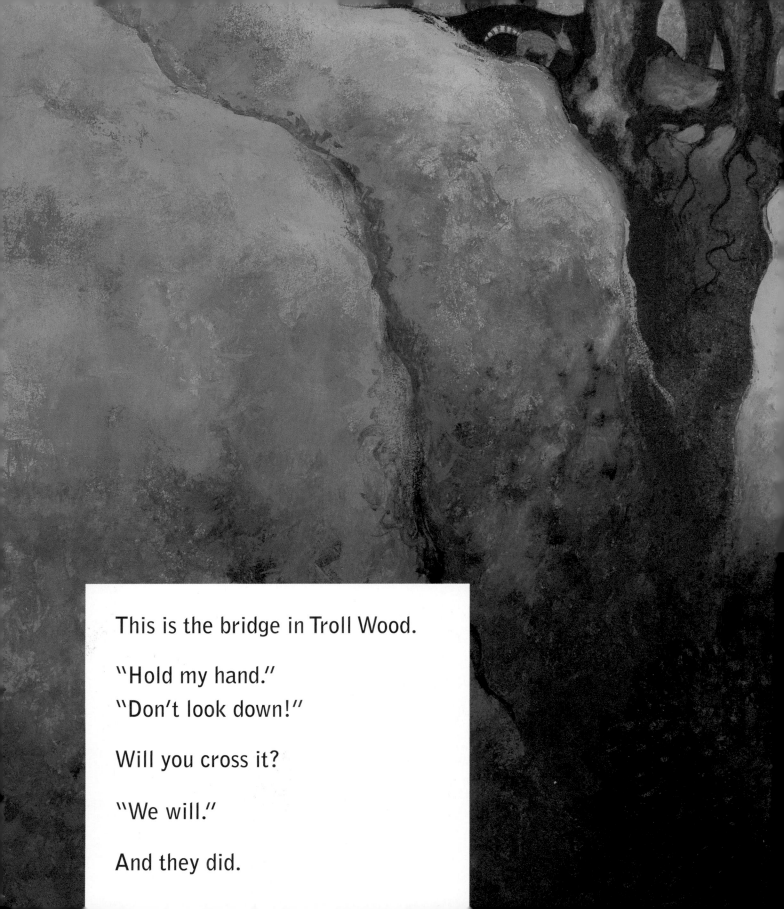

This is the bridge in Troll Wood.

"Hold my hand."
"Don't look down!"

Will you cross it?

"We will."

And they did.

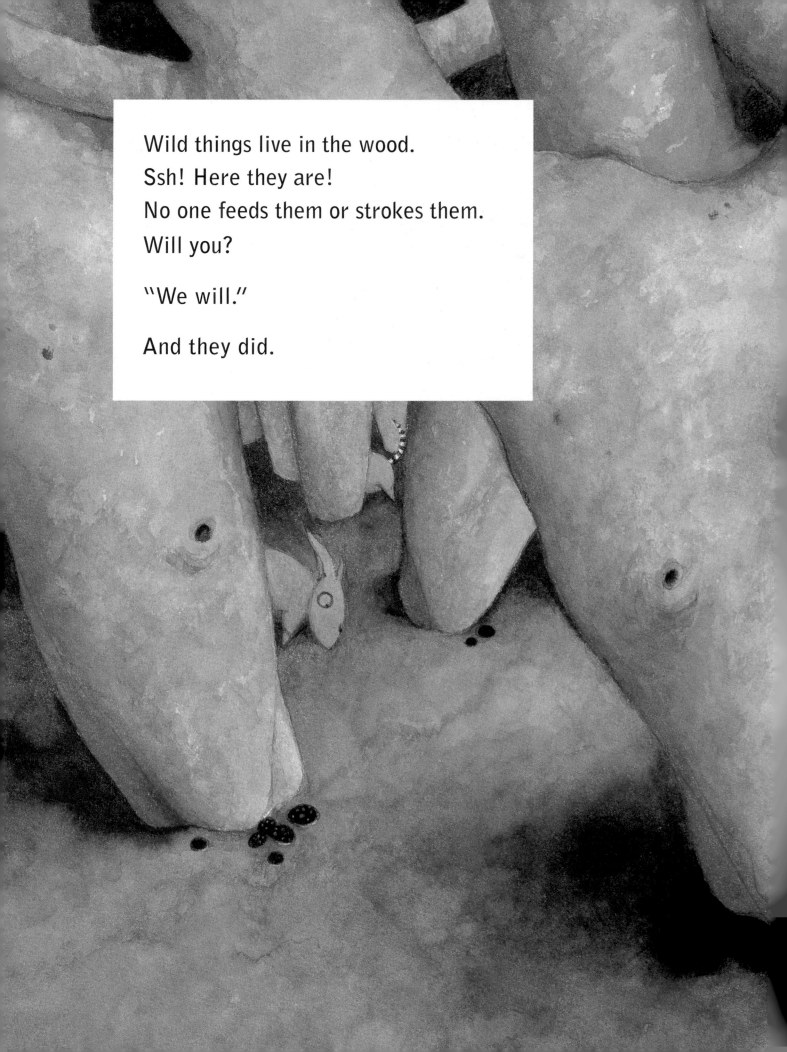

Wild things live in the wood.
Ssh! Here they are!
No one feeds them or strokes them.
Will you?

"We will."

And they did.

It's late to be lost in the wood.
Can you see the stars?
Look! There's the moon!
Will you stay here tonight?

"We will."

And they did.

Wake up! It's morning.
Time to move on.
Where are you going?
Will you know when you get there?

"We will."

And they did.

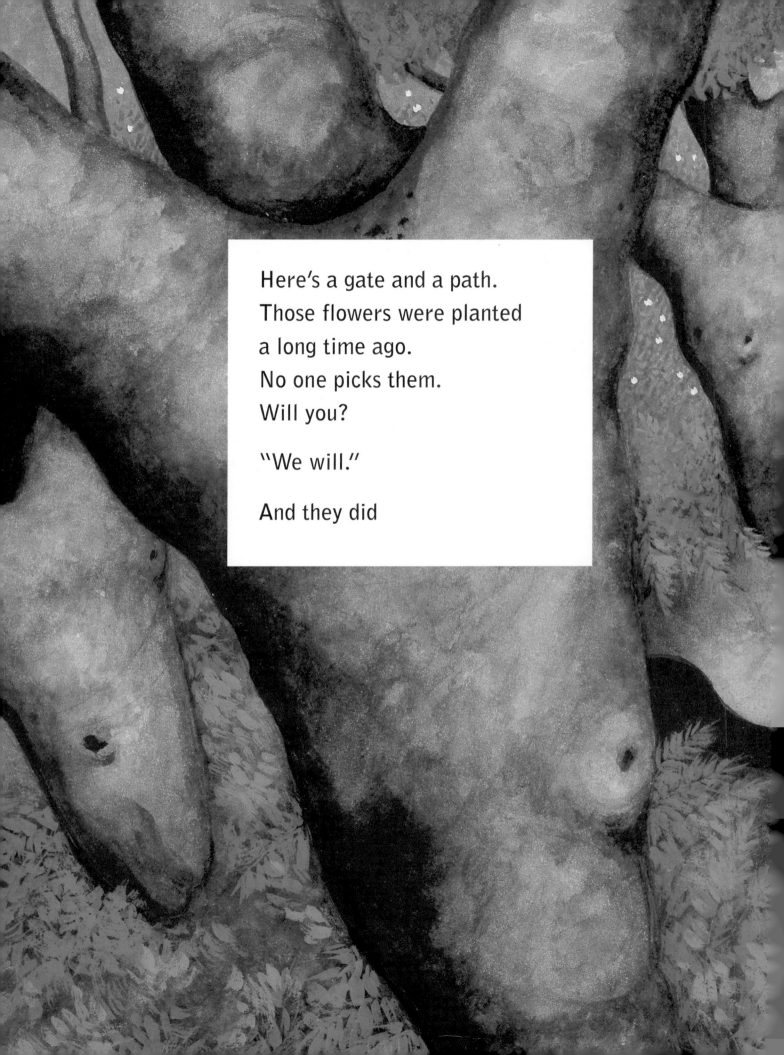

Here's a gate and a path.
Those flowers were planted
a long time ago.
No one picks them.
Will you?

"We will."

And they did

This is the house in Troll Wood.
No one lives here.
Will you?

"We will."

And they did.

"We found it. We fixed it.
We sawed and we hammered.
We polished the floor.

We scrubbed it. We swept it.
We dug and we planted.
We mended the door."

"We did it."

"WE DID IT!"

And they did.

This is the home in Troll Wood.
Will you stay here?

"We will."
"Come and see us!
We'll show you the way."

And they did.